Vera's Halloween

Vera Rosenberry

Henry Holt and Company

New York

11/12

Henry Holt and Company, LLC
Publishers since 1866
175 Fifth Avenue
New York, New York 10010
www.HenryHoltKids.com

Henry Holt® is a registered trademark of Henry Holt and Company, LLC.
Copyright © 2008 by Vera Rosenberry
All rights reserved.
Distributed in Canada by H. B. Fenn and Company Ltd.

Library of Congress Cataloging-in-Publication Data
Rosenberry, Vera.
Vera's Halloween / Vera Rosenberry.—1st ed.
p.   cm.
Summary: Vera is finally old enough to go trick-or-treating after dark and she dresses as a mummy,
but when her bandages begin to unravel, she realizes that her night is not going as she anticipated.
ISBN-13: 978-0-8050-8144-2 / ISBN-10: 0-8050-8144-5
[1. Halloween—Fiction.] I. Title.
PZ7.R719155Veh 2008   [E]—dc22   2007040898

First Edition—2008
Printed in China on acid-free paper. ∞

1 3 5 7 9 10 8 6 4 2

The artist used watercolor on Lanaquarelle paper to create the illustrations for this book.

To my granddaughter Naiya

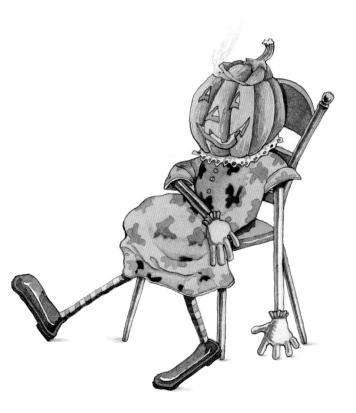

It was a perfect autumn day. Maple leaves fluttered above Vera's head as she wrapped yards of white toilet paper around her body. She dabbed red paint here and there.

Little children went trick-or-treating before dark, like Vera's baby sister, Ruthie. But this year, Vera was going out in the spooky night with her father and big sisters, June and Elaine.

At dinner, Vera's father said, "I'm almost too frightened to eat. A mummy, a bat, and a witch all in one house!" Vera was so excited she, too, could hardly eat.

Her mother handed each of the girls a brown paper bag to collect their treats. "It seems to be getting colder," Mother said. "Maybe you should all wear your winter coats."

"Mummies don't wear snowsuits!" Vera announced. "I have lots of layers of bandages, so I will be warm."

The girls rushed outside and looked back at the glowing jack-o'-lanterns
they had carved earlier that day. Vera's was the one with a fierce grin.
Father came out wearing a red cape and a devil's hat.

People were hurrying up and down the sidewalk as autumn leaves rustled underfoot. Laughing and shouting noises and ringing doorbells added to the excitement.

Mrs. Metzner gave out ginger cookies in the shape of bats.
"Just like me!" Elaine yelled, flapping her wings as she ran
down the front path.

Mr. Townsend answered his door dressed in a ghost costume. Scary music was playing and a dummy without a head sat on his porch.

One of Vera's bandages unraveled, and she had to stop and wrap it around her leg again. When she looked up, her family was gone.

Far down the street, Vera saw a red devil disappearing around the corner. She ran to catch up.

When she finally drew near, Vera realized
that it was not her father!

Vera had turned a few corners chasing the devil.
Now she didn't know where she was.

It started to rain.

Vera thought she should turn right, so she hurried in that direction.
Her bag suddenly felt light. The rain had soaked through the paper,
and her candy had fallen out the soggy bottom.

"Oh, no!" Vera sighed.

It began to sleet. Vera's wet bandages were coming off. She fixed them the best she could and walked on, hoping it was the right way home. There were hardly any children around now.

The sleet quickly turned to snow. Whirling snowflakes surrounded Vera. She wished she had put on her snowsuit, even though mummies did not wear them.

Vera saw a house with many glowing jack-o'-lanterns.
She stepped onto the porch and rang the bell. A long spooky
laugh made the hairs on her arms stand up.

Before she could run away, a giant gorilla opened the door. It filled the doorway, jumping up and down and roaring.

Then the gorilla became quiet. Vera could hear people talking inside.

"What have we here?" said the gorilla in a muffled voice. It removed its hairy head and underneath was a man. Behind him, someone said, "Apa, that's Vera, my friend from school!" This was Anand's house.

"Welcome, Vera," said Anand's father. "Ama, come quickly."

Anand's mother helped Vera inside. Anand's big sister was having a Halloween party.

"How wet and cold you must be," said Anand's mother. "Are you here alone?"

"First, I lost my father and sisters. Then I lost my candy.
Now I am lost myself," Vera said in a squeaky voice.

Anand gave Vera some dry clothes to put on while his father called her parents.

Vera drank a big mug of hot cider and ate a glazed doughnut. It was so good to be warm and dry again.

Soon, Vera's father came to the door. "At last we found you!" He had Vera's snowsuit, boots, and mittens.

"Thank you for taking good care of Vera," said Father, as he helped her bundle up.

"Here," Anand said. He pressed a big chocolate bar—the best kind—into Vera's hand from his own treat bag. "See you tomorrow."

"Thank you," Vera said, as she and her father stepped outside.

Snow lay on the ground, and
everything sparkled white. A full
moon shone in the sky. Vera's
father pulled her across the snow
on a sled.

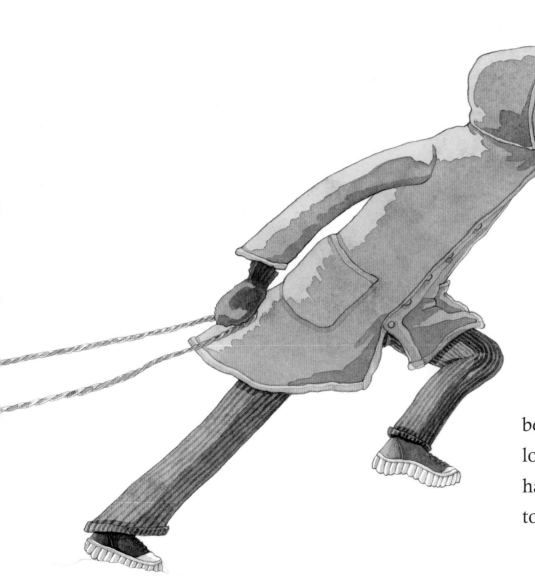

What a strange adventure this has been! Vera thought as she slid along, looking up at the stars. It was like having Halloween and Christmas together all in one amazing night.

Vera gently squeezed the chocolate bar and
snuggled down to enjoy her ride home.